Christmas

Story and pictures by **Miriam Nerlove**

ALBERT WHITMAN & COMPANY, NILES, ILLINOIS

For Anette, with special thanks to Kathy.

OTHER BOOKS BY MIRIAM NERLOVE

Easter

Halloween

Hanukkah

Passover

Thanksgiving

Library of Congress Cataloging-in-Publication Data

Nerlove, Miriam.
Christmas / story and pictures by Miriam Nerlove.
p. cm.
Summary: A rhyming text describes a girl and her family
as they prepare for Christmas, celebrate the birth of Jesus
at church services, and have a wonderful dinner with other
relatives.
ISBN 0-8075-1148-X
[1. Christmas—Fiction. 2. Stories in rhyme.] I. Title.
PZ8.3.N365Ch 1990   89-70737
[E]—dc20   CIP
                                                                    AC

Text and Illustrations © 1990 by Miriam Nerlove.
Published in 1990 by Albert Whitman & Company,
5747 West Howard Street, Niles, Illinois 60648.
Published simultaneously in Canada
by General Publishing, Limited, Toronto.
All rights reserved.
Printed in the United States of America.
10 9 8 7 6 5 4 3 2 1

I'm glad that winter comes each year,
for Christmas Day will soon be here!

I make a gift for Baby Tom
and draw some flowers for Dad and Mom.

We wrap the boxes up to hide
the good things that must wait inside.

I write to Santa and I say,
"When you come riding in your sleigh,
here's what I'd like on Christmas Day!"

We bake some cookies shaped like trains,
hearts, bells, stars, and candy canes.

Let's find a tree that's not too tall,
not too wide, and not too small.

Daddy puts the star up top.
Make sure it's on—don't let it drop!

Mom hangs our stockings in a row.
That one's mine—will Santa know?

Now Daddy must turn off the light;
I wish I could stay up all night!

Will Santa come? I try to wait
but fall asleep 'cause it's so late.

When morning comes, I run to see
what Santa left beneath our tree.

He brought us toys, some new books, too!

And here are things I made for you!

It's time to go to church and pray,
to hear how Christ was born this day.
How Joseph and Mary made their way...

so long ago to Bethlehem.
The inn there had no room for them.

Christ was born in a stable instead,
with only a manger for his bed.

In nearby fields that holy night,
some shepherds saw an angel's light.

The angel said, "Jesus is born!"
They rushed to see him Christmas morn.

Now we all sing "Silent Night."
I try to get the words just right.

The cousins come—there's lots of noise!
We play with all our brand-new toys.

Dinner's ready! I find my seat.
Our family gathers 'round to eat.

It's getting late, the stars are bright—
a Merry Christmas and good night!